P9-DEA-579

The Wishing Ball

ELISA KLEVEN

Farrar Straus Giroux • New York

To Harry, Mia, Ben, and Luna

Distributed in Canada by Douglas & McIntyre Ltd.
Color separations by Embassy Graphics
Printed and bound in the United States of America by Phoenix Color Corporation
Designed by Nancy Goldenberg
First edition, 2006
1 3 5 7 9 10 8 6 4 2

www.fsgkidsbooks.com

Library of Congress Cataloging-in-Publication Data
Kleven, Elisa.
    The wishing ball / Elisa Kleven.— 1st ed.
        p.   cm.
    Summary: A conniving crow convinces Nellie, a little cat,
that his glittery rubber ball is a magical star which she can use
to wish for a warm house, food, and a friend.
    ISBN-13: 978-0-374-38449-4
    ISBN-10: 0-374-38449-5
    [1. Cats—Fiction.   2. Wishes—Fiction.   3. Crows—Fiction.
4. Crocodiles—Fiction.   5. Balls (Sporting goods)—Fiction.]
I. Title.

PZ7.K6783875 Wi 2006
[E]—dc22
                                                    2004062605

$\mathcal{A}$ little stray cat named Nellie made her home in an old peach box.

"I like having pictures of peaches on my house," Nellie said to herself one night. "But I wish it was a warmer house, full of good things to eat. And I wish that star up there was the kind that made wishes come true."

Nellie dreamed that the star jumped down from the sky and played with her.

But in the morning Nellie was alone, her head still full of wishes and her empty stomach growling. Time to find breakfast, she thought, scrambling out into the day.

Great! A whole bottle of milk, right here.

"Scat, thief!" huffed a mother bear, shaking her broom. "That milk is for my cubs!"

"I wish I was a cub in that bear's house," Nellie said as she skittered away. She kicked a rock along the street. "And I wish this rock was a fresh, warm egg, and this puddle a saucer of soup."

And *I* wish I had a silly young cat to play tricks on, thought a crow who had heard Nellie wishing. It's been a boring morning—I could use some fun.

The crow pulled a glittery rubber ball from his nest. "Lookie here, kitty!" he called.

"What a beautiful ball!" exclaimed Nellie. "It sparkles like a star."

The crow's eyes gleamed with mischief. "It *is* a star!" he said.

Nellie tingled from her whiskers to her tail. "A star that jumped down from the sky, like the star in my dream last night?" she asked.

"Just the kind," the crow replied. "A magic star that makes wishes come true. Three wishes, to be exact."

"Is it really magic?" Nellie asked.

"It's so full of magic it can fly!" said the crow. He gave the ball a hard bounce. It seemed to shoot over the sun and back.

"Wow!" said Nellie. "But how does it make wishes come true?"

"Easy," said the crow, tossing the ball to Nellie. "Just rub this star and make three wishes. Bounce it, catch it, and your wishes will all be granted!"

Nellie rubbed the ball. She made her wishes: I wish I had a warm house. I wish I had something to eat. I wish I had a friend.

She bounced the ball, but instead of bouncing back to her . . .

. . . it rocketed off on its own.

The crow chuckled as Nellie ran after it. "Catch it, kitty! Catch it and your wishes will come true!"

"I'll catch it! I'll catch it!" yelled Nellie. She leaped for the ball, but it flashed through her paws like a slippery fish, then slid into the river with a splash.

"Oh no!" Nellie said. "My star!"

The ball bobbed and wriggled, just out of reach, struck a rock and sprang away . . .

. . . into the lap of a jowly bulldog.

Arching her back to make herself look bigger, Nellie challenged him to a game. "Hey, Dog, bet you can't throw that to me!"

"Bet I can throw it much farther!" the dog bragged, hurling the ball.

Off it sailed, over a hill, into a tree,

down to a faraway town.

Now, where did it go? Nellie wondered. Ah, here it is, shining in the grass! Nellie pounced on the shiny thing, but it was only a gum wrapper that crumpled in her paws.

Is it caught up in this tree? No, that's just an apple. Did it roll into the bakery? No, that's a sprinkly cookie.

"My beautiful little star," Nellie cried. "It couldn't have disappeared!" The clouds scowled down at her, heavy and dark. "And now it's going to rain—oh, I wish I could find it."

Nellie sniffled as she searched the sidewalk. A sunny lion, drawn with chalk, smiled up at her. What a nice lion, thought Nellie. His nose shines like a star . . .

"MY star!" Nellie said. She snatched it up.

"Oh, that's your ball?" said a young crocodile. "It made a good nose for my lion."

"But it isn't a nose, or a ball—it's a star," Nellie explained. "A star that jumped down from the sky. The crow who gave it to me said that it can make wishes come true."

"Really?" said the crocodile. "How does it work?"

"Rub it and make three wishes," said Nellie. "Bounce it, catch it—and your wishes will all come true."

"Amazing!" said the crocodile. "Can I try?"

He seemed so friendly that Nellie handed him the ball. "Just don't bounce it too hard," she warned. "It's a slippery star."

The crocodile rubbed the ball. He made three wishes,

bounced it,

and caught it, just like that.

"Okay!" he said, giving the ball back to Nellie. "When will my wishes come true?"

Nellie's empty stomach grumbled, reminding her of her own wishes. "The crow didn't tell me when the wishes would come true," she said. "I don't think it will be long, though. What did you wish for?"

"I wished that my lion would jump up off the sidewalk," the crocodile said. "I wished that I could take him home. I wished that he would roar."

Just then, a thundering roar shook the air.

"My lion!" cried the crocodile. "He's coming to life!"

But all that came was a flash of lightning and cold, spattering rain.

"I loved that lion so much!" said the crocodile, as the rain washed his drawing away. "Your ball isn't magic at all."

Nellie wanted to cry. "I wish I could make your wishes come true. I wish I could make my wishes come true. I wish I had never believed that crow." Thinking about him made Nellie so angry . . .

. . . she yowled and howled and puffed up her fur, and stuck out her sharp claws and roared.

The crocodile stopped crying. "Just like a lion!" he said.

"A hungry lion!" Nellie roared again.

"A hungry, wet lion," the crocodile said. "Want to come home and have some lunch? My mom made clam chowder this morning."

"Are you sure there's enough?" Nellie asked.

"She always makes plenty," the crocodile said. "My name is Ernst," he added.

"I'm Nellie."

At home, Ernst gave Nellie some chowder, a sandwich, an omelet, a peach, and a bowl of rice pudding with whipped cream on top.

Ernst's mother smiled as she watched Nellie eat. "Would you like to stay with us?" she asked.

"Very much," said Nellie.

When the sun broke through the clouds, Nellie and Ernst ran out
to play with the ball. They tossed it and kicked it, dribbled and bounced
it so hard . . .

. . . that it streaked away like a shooting star, into the evening sky.

"Let's wish on it," said Ernst.

Nellie wished that she and Ernst would always be friends. Ernst wished the same.

And the crow? He still wished that he had a silly little cat to play tricks on. When he spotted Nellie out playing with Ernst the next day, he swooped down for some fun.

"Hey, kitty! Did you ever catch that bouncy star?"

"Yes, I did," said Nellie. "And all of my wishes came true."

The crow eyed Nellie closely. Strange, he thought. She does look warmer and plumper. Less lonely, too.

"I caught that bouncy star, too," said Ernst. "And my wishes also came true."

"Well, well, well," the crow replied. "A magic star that makes wishes come true. I'll have to try wishing on it myself. Give it back right now."

"But we don't have it," Nellie said. "It jumped away into the sky. Maybe you'll catch it somewhere."

"I'll catch it, I'll catch it all right," the crow spluttered. He spread his wings and flew off to find it, never to be seen again.

And Nellie and Ernst? They spent a happy day together,

with many more to come.

E
KLE

Kleven, Elisa.

The wishing ball.

33910036169101

$16.00   02/14/2006

DATE			